Level 1 is ideal for children who have received some initial reading instruction. Each story is told very simply, using a small number of frequently repeated words.

Special features:

The old woman

The mother

The magic porridge pot

The little girl

6   7

Opening pages introduce key story words

Careful match between story and pictures

Once upon a time, a little girl met an old woman.

The old woman gave her a magic porridge pot.

Large, clear type

9

Educational Consultant: Geraldine Taylor
Book Banding Consultant: Kate Ruttle

A catalogue record for this book is available from the British Library

Published by Ladybird Books Ltd
80 Strand, London, WC2R ORL
A Penguin Company

012
© LADYBIRD BOOKS LTD MMX. This edition MMXIII
Ladybird, Read It Yourself and the Ladybird Logo are registered or
unregistered trademarks of Ladybird Books Limited.

ISBN: 978-0-72327-273-1

Printed in China

The Magic Porridge Pot

Illustrated by Laura Barella

The old woman

The little girl

6

The mother

The magic porridge pot

7

Once upon a time,
a little girl met an
old woman.

The old woman gave her
a magic porridge pot.

9

"Cook, little pot, cook," said the old woman.

And the little pot cooked some porridge.

11

"Stop, little pot, stop,"
said the old woman.

And the little pot
stopped cooking.

The little girl took the
magic porridge pot
to her mother.

15

"Cook, little pot, cook,"
said the little girl's mother.

And the little pot cooked
some porridge.

16

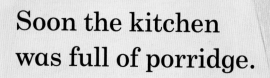

Soon the kitchen
was full of porridge.

And still the magic
porridge pot went
on cooking.

19

Soon the house was
full of porridge.

And still the magic
porridge pot went
on cooking.

21

Soon the street
was full of porridge.

And still the magic
porridge pot went
on cooking.

22

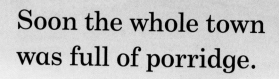

Soon the whole town
was full of porridge.

And still the magic
porridge pot went
on cooking.

25

"Stop, little pot, stop,"
said the little girl.

At last the magic
porridge pot
stopped cooking.

27

But the whole town is still eating porridge!

29

How much do you remember about the story of The Magic Porridge Pot? Answer these questions and find out!

- Who gives the magic porridge pot to the little girl?

- What does the old woman say to make the pot start cooking?

- What does the little girl say to make the pot stop cooking?